Girl Detectives

by Judith Brand

illustrated by Jeff Seaver

Harcourt

Orlando   Boston   Dallas   Chicago   San Diego

Visit *The Learning Site!*

www.harcourtschool.com

"Let's play detective," said Megan.
"Jo and I can both be detectives,
so you all go hide. Then we'll look
for clues to find you."

2

"I see some tracks in the snow," said Jo. "There are big ones and little ones. Maybe A.J. and Jim made them. Let's go!"

"I told you we would find them.
They are both here," said Jo.
"Hello, A.J. Hello, Jim. We saw
your footprints in the snow."

4

"Look," said Megan. "There's a gold yo-yo. Beth had a yo-yo." Megan pulled the yo-yo from the snow.

Megan held out the yo-yo.
"Hello, Beth," said Megan. "Here's
your yo-yo. It was a good clue!"

"Are there any tracks in the mud?"
Megan asked.

"Yes," said Jo, "but they were
made by Penny, the cat!"

"Look near the post on the porch,"
said Jo. "Look at the floor. Are
those Evan's footprints?"

"No, these footprints are too big,"
said Megan. "I think Mom made
these tracks."

"I hope we find Evan soon," Jo said. "Let's go over there, okay?"

"Something broke this branch not long ago," said Megan. "There's a piece of the branch on the snow."

"Maybe an animal broke it,"
said Jo.

"No," said Megan. "There are
footprints also. I'll show you."

Jo said, "I see the tracks. And I see Evan, too. We found lots of clues and all of our friends!"

"So do you want to play some
more?" asked Beth.
"No," said A.J. "I'm cold. Let's all
go home."

"I'm cold, too," said Megan.
"Nature is fun, but now I want
to go inside and get warm."

"I thought you'd be here," Mom
said. "This was on the floor."
Megan laughed. "Mom, you're
a detective, too!"